MIGHTY TRUCK

MUDDYMANIA!

WRITTEN BY
CHRIS BARTON

ILLUSTRATED BY
TROY CUMMINGS

HARPER

An Imprint of HarperCollins Publishers

To the mighty, superheroic
Waterhouse family
—Chris Barton

It seemed like every time Clarence was hanging out with his best friend, Bruno, another emergency came in over his secret radio.

Clarence rushed back to his pal. "All right!
Let's go! My turn to . . . oh no!"
He had missed a chance to hang with Bruno.
Clarence was *really* bummed about that.

MUDDYMANIA
TOMORROW!

But he knew a really *wheely* great way to make up for it.
Tomorrow . . .

. . . was Muddymania!

"I scored us two tickets to the biggest, messiest, muddiest event in all of Axleburg!" Clarence said.

"Muddymania!" Bruno replied. "Yes!"

"All day, buddy," Clarence promised Bruno, "it'll be just you and me."

From the get-go, the mud was flying thicker than ever.
"Flo must have worked all night making this stuff," Bruno said.

"Good old Flo," said Clarence. "She's really outdone herself."

But good old Flo was one worn-out watering truck. She was so tired that she was having trouble staying awake— and parked.

Bruno was the first to notice.
"Clarence, look!"

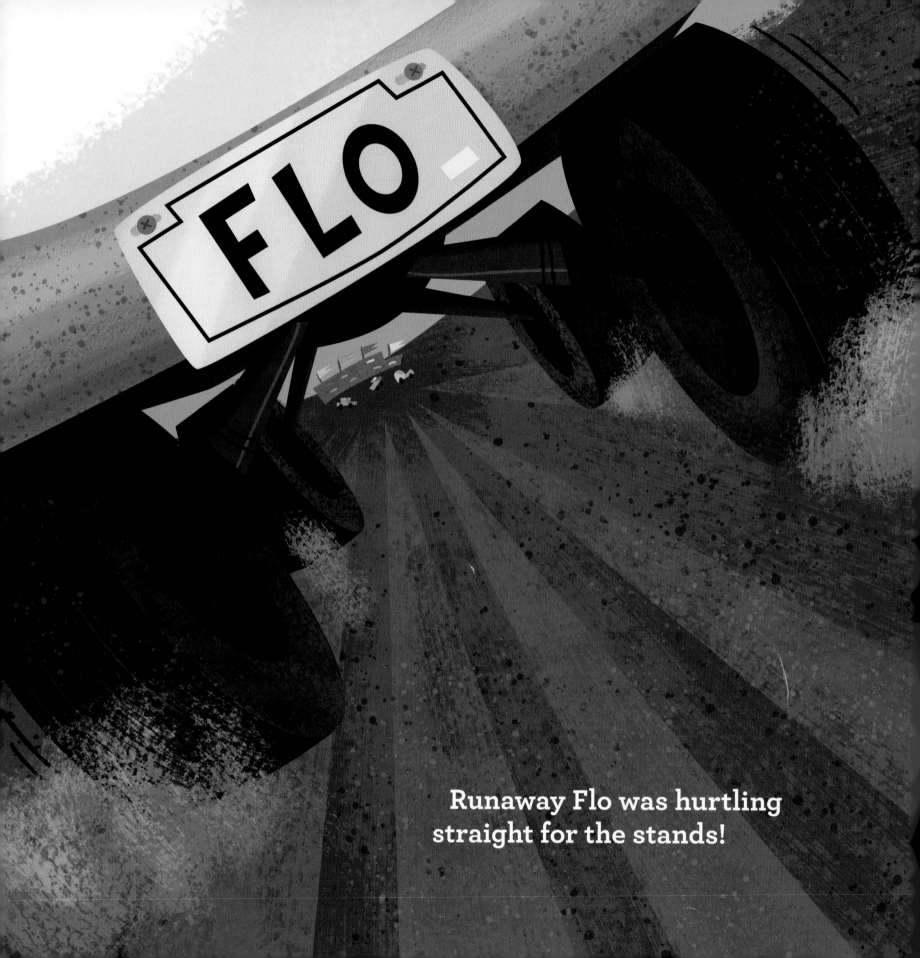

Runaway Flo was hurtling straight for the stands!

Clarence froze.
The mud. The crowd.

How could he possibly get clean, protect the
spectators, *and* keep his mighty identity a secret?

But Bruno did not hesitate.
"I bet Mighty Truck will be
there," he said. "Let's go help!"

Clarence watched his best friend
zoom off into harm's way.

"All right, let's go," Clarence said. "Gotta help Bruno!"

On his way up the hill, Clarence searched for a place to transform.

"Mighty Truck isn't here yet," Bruno said when Clarence caught up.

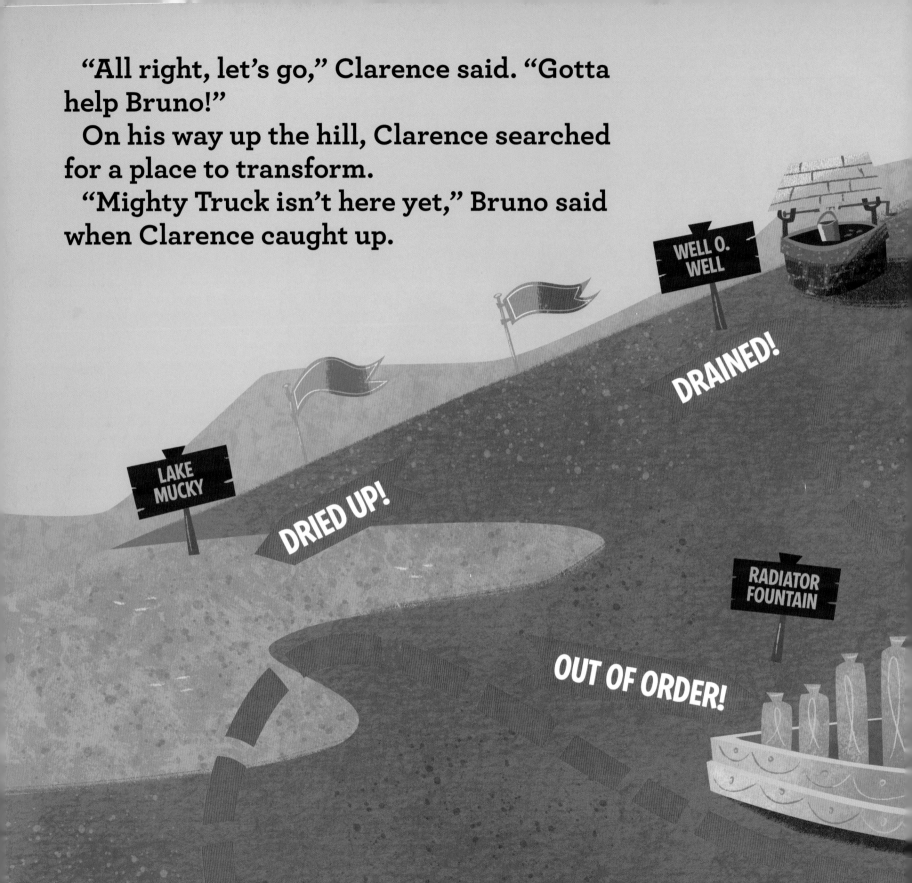

"Let's ease her away from the crowd!" Bruno said.

"Ease her?" Clarence asked.
"That won't be *easy.*"

"We need to warn the arena," Bruno yelled.
"No time," Clarence called. "Look out!"

SMASH!

"Wait! That's it," Clarence said. "Instead of a *smash*, why not a *splash*?"
He shifted into his Mighty Truck voice.
"Wake up, ma'am, and please turn on your water!"

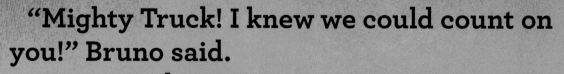

"Mighty Truck! I knew we could count on you!" Bruno said.

"You can always count on me, Bruno. Now, how about we save the day?"

"You bet!" said Bruno.

As soon as Flo was safe, she began to snooze again. Not even the cheers from the Muddymania fans could rouse her.

"We make a great team," said Mighty Truck, "but there's something I should tell you."

"You don't have to . . . *Clarence*. I already know."
"Really? How did you figure it out?"

"Oh," said Bruno, "let's just say that I knew we'd be *sticking* . . ."

"... together."